farmer

bu...der
operator

clown

lobster fishermonsters

salesmonster

doctor

street
sweeper

captain

librarian

yeoman

photographer

television
camera-
monster

automobile
mechanic

golfer

to
Doug Cushman
who paints a mean brush

Little Monster at Work

By Mercer Mayer

GOLDEN PRESS • NEW YORK

Western Publishing Company, Inc.
Racine, Wisconsin

Contents

One day, Little Monster said,
"Grandpa, Grandpa, what will I be
when I grow up?"

"Come with me," said Grandpa, "and we'll find out."

First, Little Monster helped build a road.

Next, Little Monster tried a job working with cars.

news
anchormonsters

VERY
BAD

phooey

The
GREEDY
GOURMET

MONSTER
AT THE
MOVIES

camera 3

camera 4

LATE
NEWS

EARLY
NEWS

news desk

studio
electrician

rain

snow

sun

cold

hot

100%
LOW
ACCURATE!

38°

HI

72°

300°

-4

klieg
light

Then he became a TV star.

sponsor

floor
speaker

THE RAIN
WILL BE
WET.

YESTERDAY'S
WEATHER
TODAY

TROLLUSK BROTH 3-RING

Hey, Grandpa, Lookit me.

TROLLUSK BROS. CIRCUS

CIRCUS CIRCUS

3

tightrope walkers and riders

trapeze artists

program vender

juggler

trapeze

tent pole

bareback rider

At the circus, Little Monster's clown act was a smash hit.

17

THE NEWS
You Like to Hear

darkroom

darkroom
technician

chemicals

enlarger

sportswriter

typewriter

staff artist

drawing
board

society
columnist

business analyst

editor in chief

water
cooler

copyboy

ticker tape machine

linotype
machine

delivery
monster

printing
press

RING

operator

pressmonster

screen

movie and book critic

projector

I knew it would rain.

weather columnist

With the story of his clown act on the front page, Little Monster thought he might try the newspaper business.

horoscope columnist

MONSTER NEWS

Did you see my grandson's clown act?

Extra! Read about me!

reporter

photographer

newspaper vender

19

It was time for Little Monster's check-up, so he and Grandpa went straight to the Monsterville Medical Center.

tooth doctor (dentist)

dental chair

laboratory

laboratory technician

micro-scope

happy father

happy mother

HAPPY BABY

Goo

new baby

radiologist

X-ray room

Bye-bye. You'll feel better soon.

surgical mask

SNERK OLOGIST

surgical gown

surgeon

nurse

MEDICAL CENTER

nurse

EMERGENCY

Mmmpf

BREAK IN CASE

crutches

space shuttle

solar cells

Herbie, tha Emilia Wingbat. She's fam

Explorer satellite

asteroids

ISLAND JOE'S MOON RESORT

TV transmitte

launch director

mathematician

telescope

HERMES II

lunar rover

rocket

moon wheelbarrow

astronomer

rocket technician

moon rock collector

moon science colony

launching pad

...he went to the moon,
to be an astronaut.

THE MOON

26

But he came back
to Earth for lunch.

parachute

blimp

Say, fellows, I think we're lost.

sky diver

signalmonster

flight attendant

pilot

cockpit

jet engine

oh, dear me!

BOMBANAT AIRWAYS

passenger jet

BOMBANAT AIRWAYS

I get airsick.

rotors

flight attendant

power plant mechanic

helicopter

At the airport, Little Monster visited the control tower.

"There are lots of things to do at the farmers' market," said Grandpa, so they went there next.

37

THE MONSTERVILLE OLYMPICS

target

archer

referee

basketball players

boxers

platform diver

50-meter dashers

shot-putter

STOP

caddie

Hey, Grandpa, look how strong I am!

horseshoe pitcher

JAWS

golfer

38

arm wrestlers

It just so happened that the great
Crafts Fair was going on that day.
"I love to make things, Grandpa,"
said Little Monster. "Let's take a look."

basket weaver

hand press

printer

brayer

rug maker

dye vat

dyer

forge

bellows

blacksmith

loom

anvil

weaver

yarn

knitter

41

It was time for dinner, so
Grandpa and Little Monster
headed for home.

The next day . . .

businessmonster